Murmuring Heart

Danna Colman and Thom Garrett

Illustrated by Patricia Dishmon-Caraballo

Murmuring Heart

Danna Colman and Thom Garrett

Illustrated by Patricia Dishmon–Caraballo

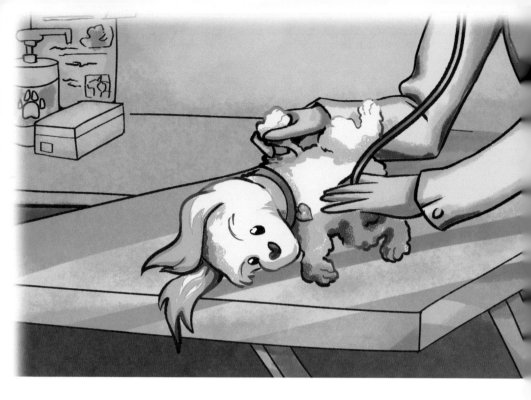

Chapter 1

Dr. Amy Brooks placed the stethoscope on the dog's chest and closed her eyes, listening intently for what they hoped she wouldn't hear. Seconds ticked by, and she repositioned the chest piece, focusing all of her attention on the telltale sounds. Suddenly the doctor's eyes flew open.

They both leaped out of their seats. "What? What is it?"

The doctor looked from the girl's eyes to the boy's, clearly taken aback by something. She put the chest piece back on the little pup's furry chest and listened again. Her eyes slowly raised to meet theirs.

"Your pup definitely has a murmur," she said slowly.

The girl dropped into her seat, tears already flowing. "Oh, no! How bad is it?"

"It's not bad at all. I can barely hear it. It's not how loud it is. It's what it's saying."

They turned to the cardiologist with identical confusion on their faces.

"Her mitral valve seems to be — Well, it seems to be saying Mommy."

"Seriously?" The boy stepped forward, and the doctor allowed him to insert the earpieces into his ears. "Wow!" he said. "You have to hear this," he said to the girl.

The girl stepped forward, reaching out a comforting hand, and then something even more unexpected happened. "Whoa!" the boy shouted.

Dr. Brooks grabbed the stethoscope out of the boy's ears and listened. "It's not saying Mommy anymore. Now it's saying, "I love you," over and over.

"Georgia!" She picked up her fluffy little bundle of fur. "Your heart murmur is talking!" And then she let out a shriek and almost dropped Georgia. Georgia was licking her like her life depended on it, and the girl said, "It changed! She's saying something else!"

The doctor grabbed for the stethoscope before the boy could get it. She listened in amazement and then passed it to the boy. Quietly, but clearly, Georgia's little heart was murmuring over and over as she kissed the girl. "I'm so happy! I'm so happy! I'm so happy!"

Dr. Brooks retrieved her stethoscope, looped it

around her neck, and then looked from the girl to the boy, her face stony. "I recommend a chest x-ray and follow-up in six months."

The girl stammered in shock. "But but but what about... what you heard?"

The doctor slammed Georgia's chart shut. "I heard a heart murmur. Nothing else." Dr. Amy Brooks turned her back to them and exited the room.

Chapter 2

Georgia was undeniably the cutest little dog in the world. She was an 8- year-old Cavapoo, a cross between a Cavalier King Charles Spaniel and a Toy Poodle, and the result was an adorable ball of creamy fur with coal black eyes and a shiny black nose perfectly shaped like a heart.

She had come to live with the girl when she was just two months old, and they had literally never been apart for more than an hour or two since. The girl took Georgia everywhere. When she sat in the dentist's chair, Georgia was in her lap. When she was at a restaurant, Georgia was cozy in her carrier at her feet. When she was attending a play or a concert, she held Georgia in her arms, usually in the front row.

The boy came later. The girl loved the boy, and so did Georgia. He, of course, loved them both, but he understood. As far as Georgia knew, she was a part of the girl, just like an arm or a leg. She was just a part that sometimes ran around, sometimes barked, sometimes slept on the boy's lap, but she was only complete when she was with the girl.

The girl flipped Georgia onto her back on the sofa and pressed her ear to her furry little chest while Georgia wriggled with delight. "I can't hear it! I can hear her heart, but I don't hear any words."

The boy sat at Georgia's head and let her lick his hand. "I think it's too quiet to hear. We'll get our own stethoscope."

"But then we can only hear her when she's lying still. Her heart murmur never stops. What if she's murmuring to us all the time, everywhere she goes? She's heart-talking to me! I want to hear it all!"

The boy was quiet, thinking. Slowly, he sorted out his thoughts. "It seems to me we could do that. I don't know exactly how, but if the sound is there, we should be able to pick it up with a microphone. And if we can do that, we should be able to amplify it through a speaker. Maybe I could rig something to her harness that has a Bluetooth mic and speaker with a little battery pack."

"Yes!" shouted the girl, pulling him in for a big kiss. "Yes! Thank you! That's perfect!"

"Whoa! Hang on! I said maybe. I don't know anything about this stuff. I don't know if it's really possible or not, but even if it is, I might not be able to do it."

"But you're smart! You'll figure it out! Thank you, thank you! Now, quick! Get up and go shopping! I can't wait to hear what she's saying!"

The boy sat at his computer. He scrolled through page after page of technical information about electronics. After more than six hours, he pushed back from his desk, stretching and rubbing his eyes. He had placed his order, including a hot glue gun and a stethoscope, and at the girl's insistence, had paid for overnight shipping.

When the box arrived, the first thing they did was unpack the stethoscope. The girl placed it in her ears and lifted Georgia into her lap. Georgia was excited by this new game, and it became clear why as soon as the girl listened to her heart.

"Treatsie! Treatsie! Treatsie!"

The girl squealed with delight. "She wants a treat!" She reached into the bowl and gave Georgia a cookie.

"Of course she does," said the boy. "She always wants a treat. This whole speaker gizmo might be a waste of time if that's all she ever says." He took his turn with the scope, shifting Georgia to his lap.

"Pee pee and poopsie! Poopsie and pee pee! Now!"

The boy jumped to his feet. Georgia raced to the door, barking, and he followed saying, "When you gotta go, you gotta go!" When the two of them returned, he said, "This gizmo is going to be worth its weight in gold."

Chapter 3

She looked like a Frankendoodle. Wires looped from her chest, where the microphone pressed against her skin. Wires looped to her back, where a battery pack rode between her shoulders. Closer to her head, almost between her ears, was a little speaker. The whole thing was constructed on her harness and cobbled together with hot glue and duct tape. Like most great scientific breakthroughs, this first effort might work, but it wasn't pretty.

The boy flipped a little metal switch, and a tiny red light turned to green. They each held their breath. He was rewarded with a tiny little voice that grew louder and louder.

"…eatsie? Treatsie? Treatsie now?"

The girl clapped and squealed! The boy jumped in the air with a whoop! Georgia began to bark and dance while her little heart shouted, "Treatsie now! Treatsie NOW! TREATSIE NOW!"

Still laughing and clapping, the girl reached into the treat bowl and pulled out a handful of cookies. She gave Georgia one, and then another, and another while Georgia danced and barked and said, "Mommy! Treatsie! I love Mommy! I love treatsie! I love Mommy!"

The girl gave Georgia a big kiss and another cookie, letting her slip to the floor. "You're going to get fat if you get a treatsie every time you ask for one."

Georgia wiggled and wagged, saying, "Mommy loves me! She gives me treatsies, and I'm going to get fat."

Georgia was having the time of her life. She was getting all of the attention they could give her. Belly rubbing, ear scratching, and lots of treats! Georgia danced around, wagging from the tip of her tail to the tip of her nose, complete with her own excited narrative.

"Do you like that, Georgia? Do you want me to scratch your back?"

"Yes! Yes! Wait, no! Ears! Not back. Ears! Yes, ears! Wait, no! Tummy! Tummy tummy tummy!"

Chapter 4

T he boy sat, lost in thought as he watched Georgia dozing on the girl's lap. It was no secret that Georgia was smart. In fact, she was one of the smartest dogs he had ever known, but she was also stubborn with what appeared to be selective hearing. Whisper the word "treatsie," and she would be at your feet in an instant, but say, "Come here," and she seemed to be deaf. He was wondering what she could be thinking, and now, for the first time, it occurred to him that he might be able to negotiate with her.

"Hey, Georgia," said the boy. "Come here!"

Nothing.

"Georgia! Come!" He clapped his hands sharply.

Georgia lifted her head lazily and turned in his direction.

"Georgia! Come! Come here!"

Georgia's voice, somehow produced by her murmuring heart and then amplified by the microphone and speaker strapped to her chest, said clearly and succinctly, "No." She laid her head down on the girl's lap and closed her eyes.

The girl looked at the boy, shaking her head. "Well, that explains a lot," she said.

"Call me old fashioned," said the boy, "but I thought dogs weren't supposed to say no to their human."

"But she's not just a dog," said the girl. "She's Georgia!"

"Right. My mistake." The boy knelt down so he could be at eye level with the fluffy ball of fur resting on the girl's lap. "Georgia? Hey, Georgia! Would you do something for me?"

This time she didn't even lift her head. "No."

"At least she seems to understand, but I think she needs a little work on her attitude."

"No," said the girl. "I think the problem is just that she really doesn't want to do what you want her to do. Ask her something else."

He thought a moment and then stood across the room from Georgia's basket of toys. He gave Georgia a cookie and said, "Now, Georgia, go get Froggy!"

"No."

The boy rolled his eyes. "Georgia, bring Froggy to me, and I'll give you a treat."

Georgia moved slowly, apparently completely disinterested, but she studied the basket, selected

Froggy and brought it back, exchanging it for a cookie.

"Really? Do you think you could look any more disinterested?"

The girl leaned forward in her seat and said, "Georgia, bring Mommy your Bunny!"

Georgia perked up and trotted to the toys, easily finding Bunny and bringing it back to her. The boy gave her a cookie, and then the girl said, "Now, quick as you can! Bring me Monkey! Quickly, Georgia! Quickly!"

Georgia sprinted over, grabbed Monkey and brought it right back, receiving another cookie.

"Faster!" said the girl. "Faster! As fast as you can! Bring me Piggy!"

Georgia was having fun now. She ran as fast as she could, saying, "Piggy Piggy Piggy!" Before she could even get a cookie, the girl was saying, "Snowman! Bring me Snowman!"

Georgia spun around and raced back, barking with excitement and saying, "Get it! Get it! Get it!"

"Now, Skunky!" shouted the girl. And then, "Squeaky Thing!" And then, "Cow!" And then, "Pink Bear!"

Georgia ran to the basket but then stopped. There were a half dozen toys, but none of them were Pink Bear. She was confused. She turned back, tipping her head to one side. "Pink Bear?"

"Where's Pink Bear?" said the girl.

"Where's Pink Bear?" said Georgia.

"Where is Pink Bear?" asked the girl again. "Can you find Pink Bear?"

Georgia looked at the toys and then turned back to the girl. "Pink Bear?"

"Think, Georgia. Think. Can you remember where Pink Bear is? Can you find Pink Bear somewhere else?"

Georgia's head tipped all the way over and then snapped straight up. With a bark, she spun

around, saying, "Pink Bear! Pink Bear! Pink Bear!" She ran into the bedroom and ran back to the girl with a tiny stuffed bear in her mouth. The girl gave her a big hug while Georgia covered her face in sloppy dog kisses.

"Do you want a treat?" said the boy.

"No treat," said Georgia. "Kisses! Kisses kisses kisses! I love Mommy! Mommy loves me! Love love love!"

Chapter 5

"Georgia! Come!" said the girl. "Mommy? Mommy Mommy Mommy!" Georgia hopped down from the sofa where she'd been napping and scampered into the kitchen.

"Good girl, Georgia. Would you like a treat?"

"Treatsie! Treatsie treatsie treatsie!"

"Would you like cookie treat or turkey treat?"

"Turkey! I love turkey! I love Mommy! Turkey!"

The girl popped the morsel into Georgia's mouth, and Georgia looked up at her and said something the girl didn't recognize.

"Georgia? What did you say?"

Georgia swallowed, sniffed around in case she had dropped any scraps and then looked up at the girl and said, "Thank you."

The girl scooped up Georgia with hugs and kisses. "Oh, Georgia! That's the sweetest thing I've ever heard! Here! Here's another!"

Georgia stood on her hind legs, just as excited as the girl. She took the treat and said, "Thank you, Mommy! Thank thank thank! You you you!"

Just then, the boy joined them in the kitchen. The girl said, "Quick! Give Georgia a treat!"

The boy did as he was told. Georgia took the treat and said, "Thank you."

"Wow! Listen to you," said the boy. "What a polite little girl you are! Here's another treat for being so polite."

Just as the boy reached into the treat jar, there was the sound of a crash coming from the street. They rushed out the door. There had been a collision right in front of their house. The boy pushed open the gate to see if there was anything he could do while the girl called 9–1–1. The patrol car was there in seconds.

The boy turned to the girl to say, "Good job," and the girl looked around. In a quiet voice, she said, "Where's Georgia?"

Georgia was gone.

Chapter 6

"Mommy?" A truck roared down the street, and Georgia ran for cover under a tree. The front door of the house opened.

"Mommy?"

An old man stepped out. He spotted Georgia and began to shout. "Hey! Get off my grass! Go on, you filthy mutt! Get out of my yard! Go on! Get lost!"

He hobbled down his front steps and started towards Georgia, menacingly stretching out his hands. He made a grab for her, and she took off like a bolt of white lightning. She ran as fast as she could for as far as she could. She ran until she was out of breath. She ran until her heart was pounding.

"MOMMY?" Her heart was hammering in her chest, working harder than ever, and that made her heart murmur much louder. "MOMMY! MOMMY! MOMMY!"

"Did you hear that?" Two women walking past on the sidewalk stopped and turned toward the cluster of shrubs where Georgia was hiding. "That sounded like a little girl. Do you think she's lost?"

"MOMMY?"

"It is! It's a little lost girl!" The two women started to push their way into the thick branches.

"MOMMY?" Georgia heard the voices and began to wag her tail. She was so scared, but now her Mommy had found her. Suddenly, the branches were swept aside and a stranger's face appeared. "NOT MOMMY!" Georgia was terrified! She raced away blindly, running into the street. Cars screeched to a stop and honked blaring horns at the little dog.

One of the women watched her go. "Look at that little dog. It's probably lost, too. Should we try to catch it?"

"Let it go," said the other. "The little girl is more important. I could've sworn I heard her right here."

Georgia ran. She ran away from the bellowing, thundering cars. She ran away from the scary people with their grabbing hands. She ran, and she ran, and she ran.

At last, when she felt like she couldn't run another step, she spotted a hiding place. It was a narrow space between two shops. It was dark and dirty, just an alley with some filthy garbage cans and trash littering the ground.

Georgia was alone and lost. She had never been alone in her life. She had hardly ever even walked around outside by herself, and she certainly had never been this dirty. Her fluffy white paws were covered with mud. Her long ears hung like rags on each side of her head. And worst of all, her tail, her gorgeous plume that she held up so proudly, now dragged behind her in the dirt.

She hid in the filthy shadows of the garbage cans, shivering and trying not to make a sound. She watched the light fade as the sun set, and soon she was enveloped in darkness.

"Mommy?" Her little heart whimpered. She

couldn't stop it, so she sat in the dark and spoke. "Mommy? Where are you? I want Mommy. I want treatsie. I want bedtime."

She heard a low rumble, a threatening growl. An enormous dog approached.

Chapter 7

Georgia crouched farther back into the shadows, trying to hide in the old boxes and smelly garbage lying between the cans. "Go away!" said her heart. "Go away! Scared scared scared!"

The big dog growled louder. It had heard. It crouched, creeping forward, stalking her, ready to pounce. It let out one sharp bark, and Georgia twitched with fear. The papers around her rustled. It had found her.

"Mommy! Pink Bear! Bedtime! Mommy!"

The other dog let loose a barrage of deafening barks, its huge teeth snapping. Unafraid, it dove head first into the darkness between the garbage cans. It grabbed whatever it could catch in its mouth. Boxes, cans, and garbage flew into the air as it howled and snapped its jaws. Georgia was paralyzed.

Then it found her, tearing away the last of the boxes. Georgia was pressed against the brick wall, too frightened to move. The enormous dog seemed to enjoy seeing her tremble. Its growl rolled like thunder in its chest while its lips curled, displaying fangs like dripping daggers. It approached slowly, inch by inch, as Georgia watched, frozen in place.

"Go away," she said. "Go away. Don't see me. Don't find me. Go away!"

With a roar, it pounced! Georgia sprang forward, and those flashing teeth snapped shut on nothing but air. Georgia ran between its legs and then deeper into the alley. The dog seemed lost for a moment, confused by its vanishing prey, but then it heard the scuffle of Georgia's paws as she desperately tried to escape. It turned and bounded after her, its long legs quickly making up the distance between them.

There was a blue dumpster ahead, mounted on wheels, leaving a little space beneath it. Georgia flew as fast as she could, diving under the dumpster just as those angry jaws snapped onto her tail. She lost some of her beautiful plume, but all the dog got was a mouthful of hair.

Georgia crawled forward while the crazed dog howled, trying to squeeze its head and shoulders under the dumpster. It scratched and scraped on the concrete, trying to force its way into the narrow space, but then Georgia popped out the other side. Up ahead, a chain link fence blocked the end of the alley, but there was a space at the bottom. Georgia would be able to slip under it, but her attacker wouldn't.

As she raced for the fence, Georgia could hear the bellowing of the hungry dog behind her. It grew louder as it approached, closing in on her again. She dove under the fence.

With a jolt, Georgia was yanked to a halt. The wire at the bottom of the fence had snagged her harness. She pressed forward and then pulled back, but she was trapped. The other dog was almost on her. Georgia lunged with all her might, and the buckle on her harness gave out. She was able to wriggle forward, barely slipping out of it, as the vicious dog howled, throwing itself over and over against the fence as it raged.

Chapter 8

Poor Georgia was cold, dirty, and scared. Back at home, sometimes a falling leaf startled her, and other times it was the mail dropping through the chute, but now for the first time in her life she was truly frightened. She trotted on through the night, too afraid to hide in the shadows again but still afraid of everything that moved. And now, because she had lost her harness, she had also lost her voice. Her heart was no longer speaking. She was completely alone.

Cars and trucks, with their deafening engines and blinding lights, roared past her in an endless, deadly stream. She ran away from the noisy street only to find another one just as full of those terrifying vehicles. She was trapped in a place she didn't like, just

buildings and streets, no grass or trees. She walked close to the brick walls, staying as far from the traffic as possible, while keeping an eye out for danger. One wrong move, and she would be dead.

Georgia followed the sidewalk as far as it went, but there was another street with its incessant rush of cars. There were people standing there, watching the cars. Georgia wanted to talk to them. She could feel her heart saying, "Mommy? Where's Mommy? I want Mommy!" but she made no sound. She just stood to the side, watching the people who were watching the cars.

Suddenly, the cars stopped, and the people just walked right out into the middle of the street! It was a crosswalk. Georgia raced to catch up and then stayed right by their feet, hoping they would protect her from the cars. It worked!

Now Georgia knew how to get past the cars, but she still didn't know where she was or where she was going. She wished Mommy would find her. Mommy always took care of her. Mommy always kept her safe. She wanted Mommy more than she'd ever wanted anything before. Maybe if she just kept walking, she'd find Mommy.

The sky turned from black to gray, and more people were walking on the sidewalks and then waiting at the edge of the streets for the cars to stop. Georgia kept away from the strangers as much as she could, but when they walked into the crosswalk, she always joined them. It was the only safe way to get across.

As the gray sky turned blue, the sidewalks became crowded with people. Georgia dodged this way and that, trying to avoid the army of marching feet, but she was kicked and bumped and sometimes stepped on. As people repeatedly stepped on her tail, her poor plume got shorter and dirtier.

She was standing behind a crowd of people waiting for the cars to stop, when she noticed more people coming up behind her. One by one, they came right up to her, surrounding her. Soon there were as many people behind her as there were in front. She was stuck in the middle, and when the cars stopped, they all started forward at once. She weaved and swerved and ducked and jumped, but still she was kicked and stepped on. Suddenly she felt a pair of hands wrap around her body, and she was plucked up and out of the path of the trampling feet.

"Mommy!" said her heart. "Mommy!" She twisted, looking back over her shoulder and saw a face she didn't know. "Not Mommy!"

Georgia tried with all her might to get away, but the stranger just gripped even tighter. She was kicking his arms with the sharp nails on her back paws, trying to make him drop her, but he held her at arm's length so she couldn't get him to let go. When they got across, he stepped to the side of the crowd and stopped, examining Georgia as she struggled to break free.

"You sure are a feisty one, aren't you, buddy?" He had a nice voice, and when Georgia stopped kicking, he spun her around to get a good look at her. "Oh, I beg your pardon, Miss. You're a girl, aren't you? And a very pretty one, too. You look like you've had a rough day or two, but I'll bet you were somebody's princess. You certainly don't belong on the street. Let's get you all cleaned up and figure out a way to get you back home."

Georgia wasn't ready to trust this man even though he had a very friendly face. She didn't understand most of what he had said, but she liked the sound of getting cleaned up, and especially of going home. And she liked that he called her pretty.

"My name's Dylan." He held her more comfortably in his arms, scratching her neck. "No collar, no tag. What should I call you?"

Dylan looked around for inspiration. They were standing at the corner of 12th Street and Olive Avenue. "A pretty girl like you needs a pretty name. How about Olivia?"

Georgia licked his arm and Dylan continued. "Olivia it is! Hey, Olivia, you must be hungry. How would you like a little treat before we get going?"

Georgia was excited! She reached up and gave the nice man a sloppy dog kiss while her heart silently called out, "Treatsie? Treatsie! Treatsie treatsie treatsie! Pink Bear! And Mommy?"

Chapter 9

Georgia was as lost as ever. She still missed her home, and she still missed her Pink Bear, and most of all, with every fiber of her being, Georgia still ached for her Mommy. Her heart, silent now to everyone except herself, called out for Mommy with every beat. Her murmuring heart was heartbroken. As bad as everything was, there was a silver lining. Georgia had been found by Dylan.

Dylan held her in his arms, and Georgia felt safe for the first time since she last saw her home. As they entered a coffee shop, they were greeted by a gruff voice.

"Yo, buddy! No dogs!"

"Therapy Dog," said Dylan.

"Yeah, right. Whatever."

The air was filled with wonderful smells, and Georgia, who had never missed a meal in her life, was ready to eat some of everything.

"I'll take a breakfast croissant. Ham and eggs."

The surly man threw it all together and wrapped it in foil. He handed it to Dylan and couldn't resist adding, "Your service dog could use a bath."

"Yeah, we get that a lot," said Dylan, who was already unwrapping the foil from the delicious smelling roll. He tore off a small bite and held it out. "Here you go, Liv. I hope you don't mind a little mayo."

Georgia didn't mind one bit. She gulped down the first bite, and then the second, and then the third, her heart saying, "Mayo mayo mayo!" as Dylan laughed, giving her more. He ripped off another piece with plenty of ham and eggs, and said, "Mind if I have a bite?"

"You know, Liv, that cranky cook gave me a good idea. I think you would make a great Therapy Dog. Let's get you cleaned up and have a good look."

They went in through the back entrance of an enormous building. Inside, people raced in all directions, some in street clothes, some in scrubs, and some in surgeons' gowns. It was chaotic, and Georgia didn't like it. She snuggled down in Dylan's arms.

"Hey, Dylan!" someone called out. "Where'd you get the drowned rat?"

"Don't you know a diamond in the rough when you see one? Wait until you see this little princess after her bath."

Georgia liked Dylan, but she wanted her Mommy and her Pink Bear.

Chapter 10

Georgia stood in the oversized utility sink as the spray of water rinsed away the second glorious cloud of soapy suds. "Rinse, repeat," Dylan had said. If he could hear her heart right now, he would hear Georgia saying, "Clean! Warm! Clean clean clean!"

The first thing he had done was feed her. After she ate her fill, Dylan lifted her into the sink. First, he rinsed her thoroughly, which she usually hated, but this time it was wonderful. The water was very warm, and when it poured down her head and her back and plume, it felt like hugs and kisses. She stood, not wanting to move a muscle, and watched as the water that ran from her hair to the drain slowly turned from black to gray to clear. Then Dylan covered her with shampoo that smelled like oatmeal, massaging it into every inch of her hair and skin, and then he rinsed the suds down the drain. Georgia had a groomer who gave her a bath every four weeks, but her groomer only shampooed her once each visit. Now, when Dylan had rinsed away all of the shampoo, he lathered her up again, taking his time as he scrubbed her ears and in between her toes, finally washing her tail until it was spotless. Georgia really, really liked Dylan.

As she basked in his attention, Georgia heard Dylan talking to people who passed. He said things like, "Yeah, a new one," and "just found her on the street," and "perfect for the kids," but she didn't know what he was talking about, and she didn't care. She was just so happy to be fed and warm and clean.

Dylan wrapped her in a fluffy, white towel and got her as dry as he could, and then he carried her to a table where she stood while he finished drying her with a blow dryer. He slipped a cozy pink sweater over her head and then added a simple leather collar with a tag that said, "Therapy Dog." Then Dylan said, "There you go, Liv. Now you're officially part of the team. Ready? There's someone I want you to meet."

He put her on the floor and walked away. Georgia watched him go, not sure what to do. She preferred to be carried. Then Dylan looked back at her over his shoulder and said, "You coming, Liv?"

Georgia took the hint and trotted after him. She followed him through a maze of halls and then up a stairway. They exited the stairwell and went down another hall, stopping at an unmarked door. Dylan put his hand on the doorknob and said, "Are you ready, Miss Liv? You're about to meet the oldest hospital Therapy Dog in San Diego."

He swung the door open and said, "Tobias, allow me to introduce you to the newest member of our team, Miss Olivia, the Street Princess. Liv, this is His Eminence, Tobias the Third."

Tobias was a hundred pounds of roly-poly, white-faced Golden Retriever. He had been lying on a beat-up, old chair that looked to be his and his alone. With some effort, he situated his arthritic old legs under his double-wide body and lowered himself gracefully to the floor. With the dignity that comes with age and royalty, he approached Georgia, who waited apprehensively. Tobias sniffed her from one end to the other and then back, and then he ceremoniously licked her ear.

"I'm glad you approve, Tobias," said Dylan. Then he swung the door open and said, "Shall we go to work?"

They strolled slowly down the hall, passed by much faster moving nurses, interns, and doctors. They stopped at a door almost hidden by dozens of flamboyantly colored pieces of art, each one the masterpiece of the moment from a child staying more than a night or two at the hospital. Dylan opened the door and was immediately greeted by cheers as youngsters with all types of tragic, life-threatening issues were suddenly filled with joy. "Tobias!" they screamed, and they gathered around the eternally patient, gentle giant as he gave each one a kiss.

"Boys and girls," called Dylan. "I want to introduce you all to someone very special." He lifted Georgia into his arms, for which she was grateful. She wasn't used to children, and she was not entirely sure that she liked them. "This is our new Therapy Dog. Her name is Olivia. She's been lost and lonely, and she needs some new friends. Do you remember your first day in the hospital and how scary everything seemed to you? Well, this is Liv's first day, and I think she's a little bit scared, too. So, I hope you will each introduce yourself to lovely Liv, but do it gently and help her to feel at home here, just like Tobias helped you."

The room went nearly silent as the children looked at Georgia and whispered back and forth about this new addition to their hospital family. One little girl with a shiny bald head stepped forward and held her hand up for Georgia to sniff.

"Hi, Olivia," she said in a nervous voice. "My name is Latoya."

Georgia sniffed, and then cautiously licked the little girl's fingers. Latoya giggled and pulled her hand back. Georgia's heart said, "Kids! I like kids! Kids kids kids!"

Chapter 11

Georgia was happy, but not really. Every day, she played with the children. Some of them were loud and wild, and some of them could barely lift a hand to pet her, but she knew they were all so

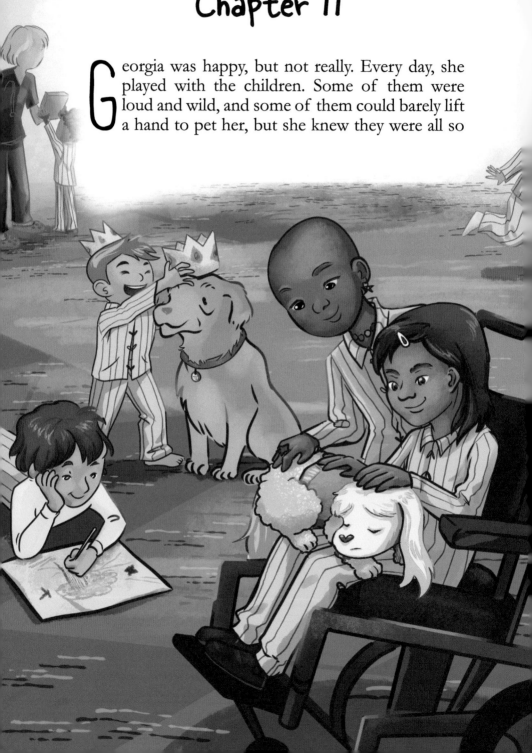

happy to see her. She also knew they were all very sick. She could smell it. So it made her happy to make the kids happy.

Every night she went home with Dylan. He lived alone in a small apartment. It was quiet and clean, and he held Georgia in his lap while he fell asleep in front of the television. Dylan had lived alone for a long time, and it made him happy to have her there. It made Georgia happy to make Dylan happy, but she wasn't really happy. Not really.

Georgia missed her Mommy. She missed her more than she could even understand. She missed her like she would miss her eyes if she were blind. She missed her like she would miss her ears if she were deaf. She missed her like she would miss her heart if one day her heart ran away and she couldn't find it. Somehow, Georgia knew that Mommy was missing her in the very same way. Her murmuring heart no longer spoke her thoughts. Day and night, it said the one thing she wanted most, her heart's desire. "Mommy?"

At the hospital, Tobias was perfect for the crowd of kids in the playroom. They could pet him, and kiss him, and even pull his tail, and he never growled or barked. Georgia, however, was not so eager to share in the crazy chaos of all those kids. She much preferred one child at a time, and because she was so small, she could climb right up into bed with them. Most days now, Dylan would leave Tobias with the kids in the playroom while he and Georgia visited the boys and girls too sick to get out of bed.

Six-year-old Billy was waiting for an operation to

fix his heart. Until then, he was bedridden. He hadn't been able to run around with his friends for over a year, and as he grew bigger, his weakened heart became more of a problem. Now it was difficult for him to even stand, so he lay in bed and waited.

Billy's door opened, and a man stuck his head in. "Hey, Billy! My name's Dylan. I have a surprise for you. Guess what it is!"

Billy looked at the man wide eyed and shrugged. Dylan pushed the door open, and Billy squealed with delight when he saw the little cream colored dog in his arms.

"This is Olivia," said Dylan, "and if you want her to, she can sit with you right on your bed. Would you like that?"

Billy reached out both arms and said, "Yes, please!"

Dylan sat Georgia on Billy's legs, and she immediately walked right up his body to lick his face. Billy laughed so hard he was helpless, squirming happily under Georgia's kisses. Dylan raised the head of the bed so Billy could sit up, but Georgia just put her paws on his shoulders and kept licking. Finally, Billy was able to get her to stop, and he hugged her while she sat on his lap.

Billy gave Georgia all the attention she could ask for. He scratched her back, and her head, and her ears. Then she rolled over so he could rub her belly, but Billy, who wanted to be a heart doctor when he grew up, didn't rub her belly. Instead, he reached for his own stethoscope to listen to her heart. He put the ear pieces in his ears, and then he held the chest piece on her chest. He listened intently, just as he had seen all of his doctors do, and then he shifted the stethoscope a few inches and listened again. He looked up at Dylan.

"She misses her Mommy," said Billy.

Dylan smiled. "Why do you say that? Do you miss your Mommy?"

"No, I just saw her, and she'll be back for dinner. But Olivia really misses her Mommy. I think she hasn't seen her in a long time."

Dylan's face showed his surprise. "You're right, Billy, but how did you know that?"

"Because she keeps asking for her."

"Do you hear her asking for her mother, Billy? Because I don't hear a thing."

"No, silly! You can't hear her without a stethoscope!"

Dylan laughed, thinking he was catching on to Billy's game. "Oh, okay. When you listen to her heart, you can hear what she wants, right?"

"I don't know," said Billy, looking a little confused. "I just hear what she's saying."

"And what is she saying?"

"She just keeps asking for her Mommy."

"Does she? Can I have a listen?

Billy handed the stethoscope to Dylan, and he took on the serious demeanor of a heart surgeon. He placed the chest piece on Georgia and nodded his head, as if agreeing with his colleague. Then he shifted it to another spot and, as he listened, his eyes and mouth opened wide with astonishment.

Chapter 12

The boy drifted, not really thinking about anything in particular. His hands seemed to move on their own, cracking the eggs and beating them, pouring them into the pan, scrambling, and then serving them onto two plates. It was evening, but eggs were the only thing the girl would eat.

For days, they had walked, calling for Georgia and posting lost dog fliers. During those days, the girl barely ate, so consumed with worry but still hopeful. Then she lost all hope and went to bed. Day after day, she refused to get up, refused to talk, and refused to eat. Finally, the boy got her to eat a few bites of egg and eventually to sit on the sofa with him as they ate.

The girl said she missed Georgia like she would

miss her eyes if she were blind, like she would miss her ears if she were deaf. She said she felt as if her heart had left her body and had run away and gotten lost. She would never be complete again without Georgia.

That night, three weeks to the day since Georgia had disappeared, the boy served the eggs and then sat on the sofa next to the girl. She took her plate with a weak smile of thanks, grateful for his patience as much as his love. The boy picked up the remote and clicked on the TV, just in time to hear the news anchor say, "Our person of the week isn't even a person, but she has something to say. You don't want to miss this!"

That was usually the boy's cue to turn off the news. Neither of them was in any mood for heartwarming stories about someone else's good fortune, but that night they had just started their eggs, so they sat through the commercials and continued in numb silence. The reporter took over the story.

"We are broadcasting live this evening from the children's ward of San Diego's Scripps Medical Center, here with Dylan Edwards. Dylan was just lending a helping hand a few weeks ago when he lifted up a muddy little dog from a busy San Diego crosswalk. From that moment, the two of them have forged a friendship, but no one could have predicted what would come next."

The girl leaned forward, her fork full of eggs halfway to her mouth.

The program switched to a shot of a man with a big dog, laughing with a crowd of children.

"Dylan works with San Diego's children, the children who have been stricken with cancer or immunodeficiency or heart defects. For years, he has given them a ray of sunshine in the form of Tobias, a good old dog who is universally loved by every child he meets. But after that chance encounter on the street, Dylan and Tobias have been joined by a new partner in their efforts to bring joy to children. Her name is Olivia."

The image on their screen switched, and the girl leaped to her feet, dropping her plate to the floor. The boy managed to set his plate aside and then stood, throwing his arms around her as she screamed and pointed at the screen. There was Georgia, loving and being loved by the children at the Scripps Medical Center.

"Wait!" said the boy. "Wait! Listen!"

A man in a white coat was speaking to the camera. He said, "She has a heart murmur, common among many breeds of dogs. But there is nothing common about hers. Hers is nothing short of a miracle. But don't take my word for it. Hear for yourself!"

There was Georgia in Dylan's arms. He gently placed her on a cushioned platform and gave her a treat. He rolled her to her back and gave her another treat. "Stay right there, Liv." A technician placed an ultrasound probe on her chest as Georgia lay still, looking anxious. Dylan spoke to her. "Liv, would you like a treat?"

From the speaker built into the ultrasound equipment, a voice said, "Treatsie? Treatsie treatsie treatsie!"

Dylan gave her a treat and asked another question. "Liv, would you like to go see Billy again?"

From the speaker, Georgia said, "Kid? I like kids! Kids kids kids!"

Then Dylan said, "Liv, would you like to go home?"

Georgia's heart said, "Home? Mommy? Mommy? Mommy! Mommy! I want home! I want Mommy! Mommy? Where is Mommy?"

Dylan lifted Georgia into his arms, hugging and kissing her. All the camera could hear now was her quiet crying, a sad dog who missed her home. Without the speaker, her voice was silent, but her heart was still calling out for Mommy.

LIVE

10

Wonder Dog at San Diego Hospital

Alex Thompson

The camera shifted to the reporter. "Veterinary and human cardiologists alike are astounded by Olivia, the dog with the talking heart. When asked for their medical opinion, they have all refused to comment. But Dylan Edwards, the man who knows her best, gave his opinion. He said she is a little dog with a heart so full of love, it just had to be expressed somehow. Back to you, David."

The girl and the boy didn't hear that part. They were already in the car, racing to the Scripps Medical Center, hoping they would soon hold Georgia in their arms again.

6:00 PM

San Diego, California

Epilogue

Their reunion was spectacular! The boy pulled into the hospital parking structure, and the girl didn't even wait for him to park. As soon as she saw the elevators, she popped her door open and jumped out of the moving car. With no empty spots in sight, he pulled into a No Parking zone and killed the engine, chasing after her in time to catch the elevator. In the lobby, they spotted the news reporter on his way out.

"Where's Georgia?" shouted the girl.

"Who's Georgia?" replied the reporter.

"Georgia! The dog! The talking dog! She's my Georgia!"

"You mean Liv? She's your dog? Stay right here, lady! I'll take you there myself!" And then he yelled out the door to the television station's news van. "Marty! Bring the camera and a mic, stat!"

The crew had a hard time keeping up with the girl who kept running ahead while the reporter tried to stop long enough to explain to the camera what was happening. They all gathered in the conference room where they had filmed the original news story. A few people were still milling around, and they looked up in surprise as the boy and the girl each grabbed a handle to open the double doors. They burst into the room, and pandemonium ensued as the happiest dog who ever lived was reunited with her Mommy, the happiest human who ever lived, and it was all filmed for broadcast on the evening news.

Two weeks later, life at home was back to normal, or at least as normal as a home with a talking dog could be. Georgia was now an international celebrity with thousands of fans who eagerly awaited her daily YouTube videos. When the boy explained to the news reporter about the harness contraption he had made, an expert in assistive technology donated a device of his own design that gave Georgia's heart a full, clear voice, and it was so small it was almost invisible. Georgia talked all day long, and her vocabulary was growing by leaps and bounds.

One day, a letter arrived addressed to Georgia. It was from Japan. The girl read it and then handed it to the boy. The look on her face was so serious it made him nervous to take the letter. It was from a veterinary cardiologist. He was offering to perform a surgery that would give Georgia many more years of healthy life.

It would also end her murmur. Her heart would be silent.

The boy dropped the letter on the table. He looked at the girl who was clearly upset, torn by the two paths that lay before her. One saved Georgia's voice, but nobody could say how fast her heart condition would deteriorate, or how it would affect her health. The other would give her a normal lifespan, but it would end the extraordinary connection they now shared through her murmuring heart.

"It's your choice," said the boy. "I can't tell you what to do. I can't even give you any advice. It's up to you."

Tears began to spill from the girl's eyes. "I don't know. I don't know what to do."

Just then, Georgia trotted into the room. "Mommy?" said her heart. "Mommy! There you are! I love you, Mommy!"

The girl lifted her up in her arms, and Georgia covered her face in sloppy kisses. "Mommy! Mommy Mommy Mommy! Love love love! I love Mommy!"

The girl was laughing and crying at the same time. "Now I know," she said. "Now I know what to do."

The girl held Georgia up so their noses were almost touching, and they looked into each other's eyes. "Georgia," she said. "I love you sooo much!"

"Mommy loves me! I love Mommy!"

The girl continued. "I know you do. And because we love one another so deeply, our hearts will speak without words." Her voice caught in her throat, and she drew Georgia in close before continuing. "We're

going to have many more years to love each other.
Isn't that wonderful?"

Georgia looked a little confused, but then she
licked the girl's nose, and the girl knew exactly what
she meant.

Printed by Amazon Italia Logistica S.r.l.
Torrazza Piemonte (TO), Italy